A NOTE TO PARENTS

When your children are ready to "step into reading," giving them the right books is as crucial as giving them the right food to eat. **Step into Reading Books** and STAR WARS® **JEDI READERS** present exciting stories and information reinforced with lively, colorful illustrations that make learning to read fun, satisfying, and worthwhile. They are priced so that acquiring an entire library of them is affordable. And they are beginning readers with a difference—they're written on five levels.

Early Step into Reading Books are designed for brand-new readers, with large type and only one or two lines of very simple text per page. **Step 1 Books** feature the same easy-to-read type as the Early Step into Reading Books, but with more words per page. **Step 2 Books** are both longer and slightly more difficult, while **Step 3 Books** introduce readers to paragraphs and fully developed plot lines. **Step 4 Books** offer exciting fiction and nonfiction for the increasingly independent reader.

The grade levels assigned to the five steps—preschool through kindergarten for the Early Books, preschool through grade 1 for Step 1, grades 1 through 3 for Step 2, grades 2 through 3 for Step 3, and grades 2 through 4 for Step 4—are intended only as guides. Some children move through all five steps very rapidly; others climb the steps over a period of several years. Either way, these books will help your child "step into reading" in style!

www.randomhouse.com/kids
www.starwars.com

Library of Congress Cataloging-in-Publication Data
Cerasini, Marc A., 1952–
Anakin's fate / by Marc Cerasini ; illustrated by John Alvin.
p. cm. — (Jedi readers. A step 4 book)
SUMMARY: Anakin Skywalker fights to believe in his dreams in spite of his day-to-day life as a slave on the planet Tatooine.
ISBN 0-375-80029-8 (trade). — ISBN 0-375-90029-2 (lib. bdg.)
[1. Science fiction.] I. Alvin, John, ill. II. Title. III. Series: Jedi readers. Step 4 book. PZ7.C3185An 1999 [Fic]—dc21 98-48534

Printed in the United States of America 10 9 8 7 6 5 4 3 2 1
STEP INTO READING is a registered trademark of Random House, Inc.

STAR WARS

EPISODE I

ANAKIN'S FATE

A Step 4 Book

by Marc Cerasini
illustrated by John Alvin

Random House
New York

THE DREAM

The yellow Podracer sped through the desert, kicking up dust. Sunlight bounced off the massive engines. Flames shot from the afterburners.

Anakin Skywalker sat at the controls. He pushed the throttle. The Pod leaped forward. It flew past the other racers and screamed across the finish line.

The other racers weren't even close.

The crowd cheered and ran onto the field. They lifted Anakin onto their shoulders and carried him to the winner's circle. A wise man and an angel were waiting for him there.

Jabba the Hutt raised Anakin's arm in victory. The cheers grew louder.

Then he heard his mother's voice. "Time to get up!"

Anakin opened his eyes, surprised to find himself in bed.

It was a dream, he realized. *What an amazing dream!*

He had finally *won* a Podrace. *But who were those strangers in my dream?* he wondered.

"Anakin! Don't be late for work!"

Anakin's smile turned into a frown.

It was just another day of work in Watto's junk shop. Another day as a slave.

But life wasn't *all* bad. He could smell something wonderful—his mother was cooking his favorite breakfast.

Anakin greeted his mother, Shmi, at the kitchen table.

As he ate, he thought about his dream.

"Are there *really* angels?" Anakin asked.

Shmi sat down next to her son. "There are so many stars that anything is possible," she said. "Even angels."

"Space pilots say angels live on the Moons of Iego," Anakin said. "They are so pretty they can make a spice pirate cry."

"Well, maybe you *will* meet an angel someday," said Shmi. "But right now, Watto will be angry at you if you're late."

Anakin hugged his mother.

"Be careful, Annie," Shmi whispered, holding him tightly. "And don't work too late."

Anakin laughed. "That's up to Watto."

Outside, Anakin met up with his best friend, Kitster. They walked together through the Mos Espa marketplace.

"I had a dream last night that I hope will come true," Anakin said.

Kitster laughed. "Dreams are for dreaming," he said. "They don't come true."

But Anakin wasn't so sure. Some of his dreams *had* come true. Maybe this one would too.

WATTO'S SHOP

"Where have you been?" Watto yelled in Toydarian when Anakin arrived. His master was excited—more excited than Anakin had ever seen him.

"I have a special chore for you!" Watto cried.

"Do you want me to fix something?" Anakin asked.

"I want you to gather trade goods," said Watto. "There's a sandcrawler at Mochat Steep."

"There are always Jawas at the Steep," Anakin said.

"But these Jawas have *Podracer* parts," Watto whispered. "From Regga the Hammerhead's Pod!"

Anakin remembered racing Watto's Pod against Regga. The Hammerhead had been winning, until Sebulba the Dug cut him off.

Regga's Podracer had been smashed so badly, the pit droids were still looking for the pieces. Regga was lucky he hadn't been hurt. He left Tatooine, vowing never to race again.

Not against Sebulba, anyway.

"I want Regga's thrusters!" demanded Watto. "Those thrusters could give us an edge."

He gave Anakin a cold stare. "With new thrusters, you might finally win a race."

Anakin had never won a race. He hadn't even finished one yet.

But he ignored Watto's insult. He was excited about the trip. Crossing the Dune Sea to trade with Jawas was an adventure!

Anakin rushed outside.

He attached a battered float sled to Watto's landspeeder and looked around for stuff to take with him to trade.

He dragged a set of hydrospanners and some spare droid parts onto the sled. Then he threw some motivators on the pile of arms and legs.

Finally, Anakin added a few jerikans to store water for the drive across the desert.

Then he spotted the vaporator cylinder.

Vaporators were used by moisture farmers to pull water from the dry air of Tatooine. Water was valuable on the desert planet.

This vaporator part was from such an old model that no one wanted it. Watto had almost melted it down for ore.

But Anakin had a strong feeling it would come in handy.

Maybe the Jawas will find a use for it, he thought. He threw the vaporator cylinder into the pile.

The float sled was loaded. But Anakin had one more stop to make before crossing the Dune Sea.

ANAKIN'S SECRETS

Anakin drove the speeder through the crowded streets of Mos Espa. He pulled up to his secret hiding place, behind the hut where he and his mother lived.

An unfinished protocol droid leaned like a rag doll against his other secret project—a half-finished Podracer. Anakin dreamed of someday racing that Pod to victory.

Anakin sighed.

A Podracer needed two engines. But he had only one. It had taken him forever to find the parts to build the first engine. He didn't know how he would build the second.

But it was still a nice dream.

Like the Podracer, the droid, named C-3PO, was half finished. He had one eye and no metal plates on his arms or legs.

Anakin was smart. He knew it was better if C-3PO and the Podracer looked worthless. If they looked valuable and Watto found them, he would take them.

Anakin had figured out many such ways to outsmart Watto—to survive life as a slave, he had to.

Anakin activated the droid. C-3PO sat up instantly.

"Good day, sir," C-3PO said. His voice sounded rusty.

"Are you ready for a trip to the Dune Sea?" Anakin asked. "You remember how to speak Jawa, right?"

C-3PO waved his arms. "Of course, sir! I am familiar with over six million forms of communication."

"Good," Anakin replied. "You're coming with me to Mochat Steep. You can help me trade with the Jawas."

"Oh, dear," C-3PO said nervously. "Aren't Jawas dangerous? And there are no lubricants on the Dune Sea. Without lubricants I could deactivate—forever!"

"Don't worry," Anakin laughed. "You'll be fine. I have everything we'll need for the trip."

They walked to the landspeeder. Anakin put on his goggles and got behind the wheel.

At last they were off to the Dune Sea!

THE JAWAS

C-3PO talked on and on. Anakin didn't mind. The droid spent most of the time shut down, so he made up for it by talking nonstop when he was activated.

The desert wind blew on Anakin's face. The twin suns of Tatooine burned his skin.

But Anakin enjoyed the trip. There were many wonders to see.

A herd of banthas lumbered among the dunes. The bleached skull of a desert worm cracked in the heat. And a line of Tusken Raiders rode in the distance.

After a time, they reached Mochat Steep.

Mochat Steep was a high rock formation that could be seen for miles. In its shadow, a huge sandcrawler sat alone.

"Hurry up!" Anakin said to C-3PO as they walked to the sandcrawler.

"My joints are getting stiff from the heat," C-3PO complained.

The Jawas chattered and pointed at the droids lined up for trade. But there were no Podracer parts anywhere.

There was a dented and scratched battle droid and a green astromech droid with faded paint and a broken motivator. Anakin spotted a DUM-4 droid, but Watto already had a couple of those.

Anakin asked one of the Jawas if they had anything else, but he just waved his arms at the line of battered droids.

Anakin turned to his own droid.

"I haven't heard the Jawas say anything about Regga's Podracer. Have you?" Anakin whispered.

C-3PO wandered near the head Jawas and listened closely.

"They have the thrusters," C-3PO said, returning to Anakin. "But I'm afraid they want a large sum of money for them."

Anakin frowned. He didn't have any money. And Watto was too cheap to buy parts anyway. Not when he could trade junk for them.

Anakin was good at bargaining with Jawas. But this time they were stubborn.

He told them all he wanted were the thrusters. He offered both the motivator and the hydrospanners in trade. But he could not get the Jawas to change their minds.

A Jawa tugged at Anakin's sleeve and chattered.

"He wants those!" C-3PO said. "Your jerikans for their DUM-4 droid."

Anakin was surprised. Jerikans were useful, but not as valuable as a droid. Why would Jawas want jerikans enough to make a bad deal?

Suddenly, Anakin knew how to change the Jawas' minds. He walked back to the float sled.

"Are we leaving, sir?" C-3PO asked. "I do hope so. All this sand is ruining my joints!"

Anakin ignored C-3PO and picked through the parts on his sled until he found the vaporator cylinder. He made sure the Jawas saw it.

The Jawas began to chatter and wave their arms.

"They seem very interested in that vaporator cylinder," said C-3PO.

Anakin smiled. "I knew they would be."

"Why, sir?" the droid asked.

"Because it isn't the jerikans the Jawas want," Anakin said. "It's the water inside them."

Anakin soon learned he was right. The Jawas needed water badly. The moisture vaporator in their sandcrawler had broken down.

Now each of them wanted something from the other. The Jawas wanted the vaporator cylinder. And they were willing to trade the thrusters for it. But there was a problem.

"The Jawas aren't sure they can make such an old vaporator cylinder work," said C-3PO.

"*I'll* make it work," Anakin said. "Tell the Jawas that I will make all the repairs in trade for the rest of Regga's Podracer."

The Jawas got very excited. The Jawa leader waved Anakin forward.

Anakin grabbed his tool box. The Jawas lifted the vaporator part off the float sled, and they all boarded the sandcrawler.

THE SANDCRAWLER

The sandcrawler's main hangar was huge! When Anakin spoke, his voice echoed off the walls. And, boy, did it stink! Anakin had forgotten how smelly Jawas could be. But he was excited. He had never been in a sandcrawler before.

Once inside, C-3PO stopped in his tracks.

"Oh, my!" the droid moaned.

He had spotted the droid assembly line.

Some droids were missing arms or legs. Others had no heads. Most were deactivated.

"I don't think I like this place!" C-3PO said.

"It's okay, C-3PO," Anakin said. "I'm not here to trade *you!*"

The Jawa leader led them through a hatch and down tunnels filled with steam. Here the sandcrawler was a maze of pipes. They walked past the sandcrawler's huge engines and finally reached the broken vaporator.

Anakin looked it over. Then he went to work installing Watto's old vaporator cylinder.

As Anakin tinkered with the machine, the Jawas whispered among themselves.

At last, Anakin activated the replacement cylinder. Within minutes, fresh water was dripping into the Jawas' jerikans.

"All fixed," Anakin said.

The Jawas chirped and jumped up and down.

"They say their vaporator is working better than it ever had before," C-3PO said.

Anakin was glad to have helped the Jawas. The Dune Sea was a dangerous place without water.

Anakin returned to his landspeeder.

A group of Jawas was loading Regga's thrusters onto the float sled. As they had agreed, the Jawas gave him the rest of Regga's Podracer, too. It was Anakin's payment for fixing their vaporator.

When Anakin saw that the trade included a Podracer engine, he could hardly believe it! *A whole engine!* It was scratched and dented, but he was *sure* he could make it work.

Yippee! Watto had only wanted the thrusters, and Anakin had gotten those for him. Now he had earned something for himself, too.

Anakin noticed the twin suns were setting. He and C-3PO thanked the Jawas and said good-bye.

I'm glad I trusted my feelings about that vaporator cylinder, Anakin thought happily. *Now I've got the Podracer engine I need!*

It was dark when they got back to town. Anakin hid the Podracer engine in his secret place.

"Good night, C-3PO," Anakin said. "Thanks for the help."

"My pleasure," the droid replied.

Anakin deactivated him. C-3PO sank into the corner.

Watto was waiting for Anakin at the junk shop.

The Toydarian was beside himself when he saw the thrusters.

"You traded that worthless vaporator cylinder for Regga's thrusters?" Watto said in amazement. He loved a good deal.

"I'll make a merchant of you yet!" Watto cried.

Then Watto sent Anakin home. But not before giving him more work to do.

"Put those thrusters on my Podracer tomorrow," Watto said. "You'll be flying in the next race."

THE RACE

It was the day of the race.

The twin suns shone brightly in the sky. The stands were packed with cheering crowds.

Podracers were gathering at the starting line.

Anakin was in front of Watto's Podracer, complete with new thrusters. Sebulba's Podracer was parked right next to Anakin.

"Why do humans dream they can race Pods?" Sebulba hissed in his language. "Humans don't have enough arms or eyes. Not enough *brains*, either."

"Just wait, Sebulba," Anakin replied. "I have a surprise for you."

"Do you mean Regga's old thrusters?" The Dug laughed. "I recognize them. The thrusters didn't help Regga. And they won't help *you*."

Sebulba fixed Anakin with an evil glare.

"I have a surprise for you, too," Sebulba snarled. "You'll find out just what it is at the arch to Bimmira Canyon."

Anakin tried not to let the Dug bother him, but it was hard.

Sebulba was a bully. Anakin knew that bullies were cowards at heart. But he also knew that Sebulba had a mean streak. The only way to beat Sebulba was to get to the arch first.

The pit droids moved away from the Podracers. Powerful engines roared to life, and the crowd went wild.

Anakin shut out all the sights and sounds around him. He stared at the red signal light. When it changed to green, the race would begin.

Anakin reached out with his mind. He touched the circuits inside the light. He could feel the electrical forces flowing inside it.

Then Anakin felt a surge of power.

The light turned green, and at that same instant, Anakin pushed the throttle forward.

He was off!

Anakin's Podracer rocketed across the desert. The land blurred around him. He fed fuel into the engines, and the Pod sped even faster.

Soon Anakin could see the stone arch at Bimmira Canyon. *I must reach it first,* he thought.

The engines surged with power. Anakin held on, guiding the Podracer expertly as he blasted through the arch ahead of the others.

Anakin laughed. Sebulba had missed his chance to play his dirty trick. The Dug

would just have to beat him fair and square.

Anakin roared into the canyon and zoomed between the rock walls.

Maybe this is the race in my dream, he thought. *Maybe this time I will win.*

Suddenly, Anakin saw a Podracer flash past him. It was Sebulba! He had let his guard down, and now the Dug was in the lead.

Anakin tried to pass Sebulba, but another Podracer passed his. It was Rimkar's bubble Pod.

Now Anakin was in third place.

Anakin wanted to pass the other two, but he knew the canyon was too narrow. He decided to wait until they reached Metta Drop. When they dove into the Drop, Anakin would use the new thrusters. With the extra speed, he would take the lead again.

Sebulba was still in the lead when they reached Metta Drop. Rimkar and Anakin were right behind him.

The Podracers dove into the canyon.

Suddenly, Anakin sensed trouble. He jerked the controls just seconds before Sebulba blasted his afterburners at Watto's Podracer.

Instead, the Dug's blast hit Rimkar's Podracer full on. The bubble Pod slammed into the cliff, exploding in a mighty crash.

Anakin almost got blasted! His instincts had warned him of Sebulba's trick just in time. But he was losing control. Anakin cut the power to the engines and veered off the racetrack, spinning wildly.

The Podracer skidded to a stop in the sand. Anakin climbed out of the wrecked Pod, covered in dust.

He watched as Sebulba crossed the finish line, winning the race.

I lost! Anakin thought sadly. *Maybe Kitster was right—dreams are for dreaming, but they don't come true.*

THE SPACE PILOT

"Sebulba cheated," Anakin said.

"Of course he cheated!" Watto yelled. "*You* should try cheating. You might finish a race for once!"

Watto was angry about his wrecked Podracer.

"Fix that Pod, boy!" he commanded. "I want you to keep working until dark."

As the Tatooine suns sank low, Anakin worked on Watto's Podracer. His thoughts were gloomy.

I'm worse than a loser. I didn't even finish the race!

Then he heard someone calling him.

"Great race, Annie!"

His friends Kitster and Seek had sneaked into the junkyard.

"Is Watto around?" Seek asked nervously.

"No," Anakin answered. "But he told me to work until it got dark."

"It looks pretty dark to me," said Kitster. "Let's go to the market. A cold ruby bliel will cheer you up."

The boys sipped their sweet drinks and listened in on the pilots talking. Tales of far-off adventure usually filled Anakin with wonder. Now they only made him sad.

I'll never see the stars, Anakin thought. *That's just another silly dream that won't come true.*

"Those ruby bliels look tasty," a friendly space pilot said. Then he studied Anakin for a minute.

"You're the kid who flew in the Podrace today," said the pilot.

Anakin nodded.

"You've got talent," the pilot said. "More than I've ever seen."

Anakin was surprised. Watto was always telling him how bad he was. Now a space pilot was telling him he was *good!*

"I've been all over the universe," the pilot went on. "But I've never seen a human skillful enough to race a Pod."

"It's just something I can do," Anakin replied.

"When I was your age, I couldn't even drive a landspeeder," the spacer confessed. "But I still dreamed of becoming a pilot."

"How did you do it?" Kitster asked.

The pilot smiled. "It took hard work. But I stuck to it."

"Do you think I could ever be a space pilot?" Anakin asked.

"If you can fly a Podracer, you can become a pilot," the spacer replied.

"But how could Anakin be a pilot?" Seek asked. "He's just a slave."

"In this life, you can do *lots* of things," the pilot said. "How you end up is up to you."

The man rested his hand on Anakin's shoulder and looked into the boy's eyes.

"You have to trust your dreams," he said. "Or they'll never come true. But dreams are funny. Even when they come true, it's never how you *think* they will."

The pilot laughed. "There are always a few surprises along the way."

Anakin thought about the man's words. Maybe the pilot was right.

Is he the wise man from my dream? wondered Anakin. *Or haven't I met him yet?*

Anakin would just have to wait and see, and trust that his dreams would someday come true. After all, now he had *two* Podracer engines. Someday he might just race his very own Pod to victory.

"Who knows?" Anakin said. "Maybe I'll even meet an angel!"